DIARY OF A
Rugby Champ

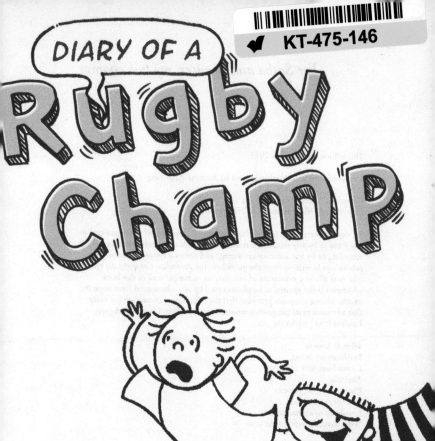

Shamini Flint

Illustrated by Sally Heinrich

ALLEN&UNWIN
SYDNEY · MELBOURNE · AUCKLAND · LONDON

For Sasha and Spencer, my two champs

This edition published in 2013

First published in Singapore in 2012 by Sunbear Publishing

Copyright © Text, Shamini Flint 2012
Copyright © Illustrations, Sally Heinrich 2012

Allen & Unwin
83 Alexander Street
Crows Nest NSW 2065
Australia
Phone: (612) 8425 0100
Fax: (612) 9906 2218
Email: info@allenandunwin.com
Web: www.allenandunwin.com

A Cataloguing-in-Publication entry is available
from the National Library of Australia
www.trove.nla.gov.au

ISBN 978 1 74331 359 6

Text design by Sally Heinrich
Cover design by Jaime Harrison
Set in 10/14 pt Comic Sans

This book was printed in August 2017 by SOS Print + Media Group,
63-65 Burrows Road, Alexandria, NSW 2015, Australia.

20 19 18 17 16 15 14 13

About the Author

Shamini Flint lives in Singapore with her husband and two children. She is an ex-lawyer, ex-lecturer, stay-at-home mum and writer. She loves rugby!

www.shaminiflint.com

<u>MY RUGBY DIARY</u>

Okay – I get it.

I really do.

I'm not a
complete idiot.

Sport is dangerous.

      VERY DANGEROUS!

      VERY, VERY DANGEROUS!!!

Sport is as dangerous as ...

falling into the lion
enclosure at the
zoo ...

OR

not looking right, left and right again when
crossing the road ...

1

OR stealing JT's lunch! (JT is the school bully. The thing he wants to do most in the world is rearrange my face.)

JT →   MARCUS

Anyway, sport is dangerous.

You could get injured.

Even worse, I could get injured.

In fact, I get injured OFTEN!!!

I remember when Dad made me play soccer ...

I was kicked.

sorry

2

I was tripped.

I was hit.

And that doesn't even include being embarrassed
(when I scored that goal with my you-know-what).

GOAL!!!

3

And what about that time Dad made me play cricket?

I wore body armour!

And I still got hurt ...

I was hit.

That was it – I got hit by the ball ...

BUT LET ME COUNT THE WAYS!!!

4

At least with cricket and soccer you're not supposed to get hit (or hurt).

If you are injured it's an ACCIDENT.

Like tripping over the carpet ...

Or slamming your fingers in the bathroom door ...

Or being struck by lightning ...

Well, getting injured in soccer or cricket is an accident unless it's the coach who's after you because you messed up.

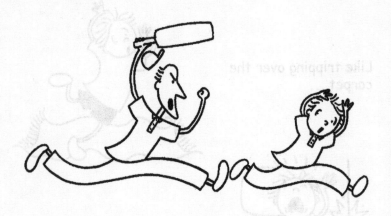

But usually, it's an ACCIDENT.

But now ...

Dad wants me to play rugby!

RUGBY!!

RUGBY!!!

My name is Marcus Atkinson and there is one thing I know for a fact:

I DON'T WANT TO PLAY RUGBY!

Is he completely bonkers?

7

Does he secretly hate me?

Has he been reading his own book?

Dad's written a book called *Pull Yourself Up by Your Own Bootstraps!*

It's really DUMB!

There's stuff in it like: 'SUCCESS is like eating CHEESE ... EASY!'

What if you don't like cheese?

When I write a book, I'll say: 'SUCCESS is like eating ICE CREAM ... EASY!'

More people like ice cream than cheese.

I like ice cream more than cheese.

Or I'll write: 'SUCCESS is like eating BROCCOLI ... really, really HARD!'

At least that would be TRUE!

Anyway, Dad's lost it. He wants me to play rugby.

Rugby is like eating cheese-easy!

Rugby is different from soccer and cricket.

In soccer and cricket, you get hurt by accident.

In rugby, they hurt you on purpose!

On purpose!!

ON PURPOSE!!

ON PURPOSE!!!

ON PURPOSE!

What's the matter with these people?

You see, Dad is convinced that I'm good at sport. He thinks the problem is that we haven't found the right game ... YET.

So far, we've tried soccer (details in my *Diary of a Soccer Star*) ...

and cricket (details in my *Diary of a Cricket God*).

And now he's certain rugby is my game.

Time to start another diary.

I expect this diary will be very short.

the very short Diary of Marcus Atkihson age 9

1. played rugby
2. Got killed

THE END ?

I tried talking to Dad.

13

I BELIEVE ...

I can stop a charging rhino – WITH MY MIND!

Or a herd of stampeding elephants – WITH MY MIND!

Or a great white shark – WITH MY MIND!!!

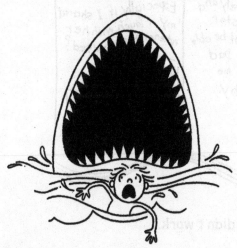

I'm dead meat.

My sister Gemma likes to stick post-it notes
in my diaries. I used to try hiding
the diary.

But it's no use.

She's too good at finding it ...

DIARY ENTRY:

Well – that didn't work.

Now what?

Rugby training, that's what!

17

What sort of father asks his nine-year-old son to risk DEATH playing with these guys?

Even Spot doesn't like them. GRRRR!

He's probably worried Dad is going to make him play dog rugby with a bunch of very big dogs.

Obviously, I didn't say any of that aloud.
I'm not dumb.

How much is Dad paying this guy?

You'd think the coach would know that balls are ROUND! Duh.

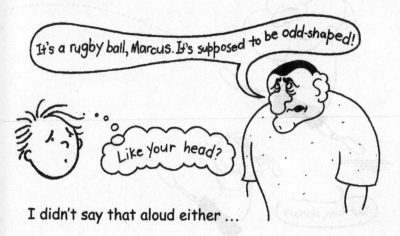

I didn't say that aloud either ...

RUGBY LESSON NO. 2

22

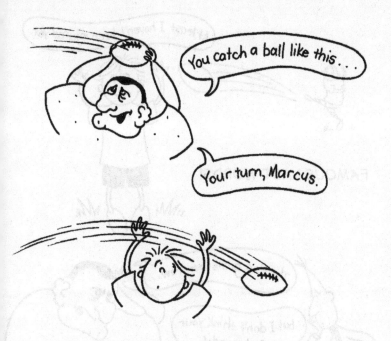

It's like trying to catch a grasshopper.
A grasshopper who has had too much coffee.
And too many sweets. And likes discos.

For once, even Dad didn't argue with Coach.

I met some of the rugby players ...

Maybe they're from
Ancient Egypt?

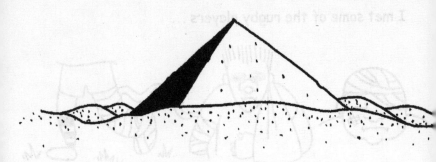

Maybe they usually live in pyramids?

Maybe they're the UNDEAD!!!

HELP!!!

26

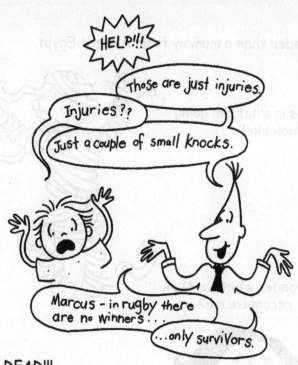

I'm DEAD!!!

Deader than a bug on a windscreen ...

Deader than a dodo ...

Deader than a mummy from Ancient Egypt.

This is what I'm going
to look like!

I wonder whether Mum
will recognise me?

Gemma will think it's
funny.

Harriet will probably
have nightmares.

Coach, has anyone ever been really injured playing rugby?

Yes, Marcus. There have been some deaths and injuries...

...but none of them serious.

I need whatever he's taking ...

RUGBY LESSON NO. 3

One of the large fellows without a neck actually tried to help me out. I think his name is Tank.

Well, that was as clear as mud.
Anyway, it doesn't really matter because I won't
be TRYING or SCORING, will I?

Apparently it's five points for a try.

And two points for a conversion.

Conversion to what?

A superhero?

A villain??

A smurf???

32

Later, Dad told me a conversion meant kicking the ball between the uprights and over the cross bar after a try.

I'm not going to score a conversion either, am I?

Marcus, when you get the ball, run with it.

Okay, Coach.

There was no way I was going to get hit again. It was time to run.

And run!

AND RUN!!!

I remembered what Tank had said. Run to the end and put the ball down and it's a GOAL! I mean TRY!

EASY! As easy as eating ice cream!!

Spot really doesn't like it when I get tackled.

That makes two of us.

Well, I suppose the good thing is that things can't get any worse.

Kids, I'd like you to meet your new team-mate.

...JT.

Marcus, I believe you already know JT?

JT?
JT is in the team?
JT IS IN THE TEAM???

I'm finished.
JT is the SCHOOL BULLY!!!

The rugby injuries will be nothing compared to what he'll do to me.

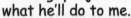

JT has spent his entire school life picking on me.

Like the time he tied my shoelaces together during basketball practice.

No prizes for guessing what happened!

Or when he glued me to the photocopier in the school office ...

and stuck pictures of my famous bottom all over the school.

Or when he left a note for Lucy (the most popular girl at school) saying that she had nice legs – and signed it with my name!

Maybe if I pinch myself really hard, I'll wake up from this nightmare.

OWWW!

Nope, didn't work.

Friendly? I'd rather be friendly to a crocodile.

I'm sure in his heart
he's a good kid.

In his heart?
In his HEART??
IN HIS HEART???

JT doesn't have a heart, Dad.
Just two fists with my name on the knuckles!!!

Why can't I be more like JT???

Later, Dad told me that Jonah Lomu, Jonny Wilkinson and Manu Tuilagi are all great rugby players. Right.

Most of the time during rugby practice, I don't understand what anyone is saying ...

The Lions were rubbish this year!

Why are we talking about lions?

I'm a Wallabies fan.

Isn't that some sort of kangaroo?

I love the Springboks.

Isn't that some sort of deer?

I'm going to be an All Black.

What does that even mean?

Hey Marcus, I guess your team is the All Black and Blues!!

Hey! Just so you know, some of my bruises are yellow and purple as well.

Later, Dad told me that the Wallabies are the Australian rugby team, the Springboks are from South Africa, the Lions are British and the All Blacks are from New Zealand. Go figure.

I think it's fair to say that Coach has taken one too many tackles in his life. Nothing he says makes sense ...

I didn't say that out loud.
I just did the push-ups.

RUGBY LESSON NO. 5

A scrum?

At the back of a scrum?

He wants me to put my head next to all those bottoms?

Is he completely mad?

Could things get any worse?
I spent the day with my head next to JT's bottom.

That DOES sound bad!
Gemma

Let's practise line-outs.

What's that?

The players line up in two rows and someone has to throw the ball in straight.

We need a code so that the other team won't guess who's jumping for the catch.

Errr! How about the first player is 1, the second player is 2...

Let me guess, the third player is 3?
That should fool them.

What planet am I on?

Great plan, Tuff.
We'll use it.

We have a game tomorrow!
I'm not worried.
We have sixteen players. We only need fifteen.
Phew!

I'd rather be a chicken than DEAD! So there.

The other team is short of a player.

Can we borrow one of your players for the game?

Disaster!

MEGA DISASTER!!

MEGA MEGA DISASTER!!!

Any volunteers?

Marcus!!

Good idea!

Thanks, team.

I won't pretend I played well.

Dad didn't look happy.

The other team didn't look happy.

Even Spot looked embarrassed.

The crowd got on my back.

Hey, Cinderella! What are you doing?

Cinderella?

Because you're always running away from the ball!!!!

Only Coach looked happy. I guess because I wasn't playing for his team.

CINDERELLA! CINDERELLA!! CINDERELLA!!!

JT was brilliant.

He scored three tries and kicked two penalties.

He tackled me seventeen times. Usually, he didn't wait to see if I had the ball.

The next day, the school newspaper had a story about Marcus 'Cinderella' Atkinson.

They even managed to Photoshop a picture.

You know the drill.

Time to spend an awful lot of time in my room with a paper bag over my head.

I need to get out of rugby training.

Coach, I can't come in today. I've caught a cold.

Makes a change when you CATCH something, Marcus!

Very funny.

My friends came to visit.
Lizzie is my friend from soccer. She's still wearing her Liverpool shirt. I don't think she ever changes ... unless she has Liverpool pyjamas.

Hari Sreenivasan is my friend from cricket. He's a wizard with the bat.

I showed him my bruises.

How come everyone is good at sport except me?

Well, I suppose there's
my best friend, James.
He's hopeless at sport.
So his dad doesn't make
him do any.

Instead, he gets to
download an app on his
iTouch every time he
gets an 'A' in Maths.

Dad says he'll let me
download some games if I score a TRY
in a rugby game.

I guess I shouldn't hold my breath ...

PIGS WILL FLY FIRST!!!

I NEED A PLAN!!!

And I've got one ...

There's only one thing to do.
I'll run away from home.

Maybe I'll become a sailor!

Maybe not.

Maybe I'll become an explorer!

Maybe not.

Maybe I'll become a fireman!

Maybe not.

I guess I can't run away. It would upset Dad too much. And Mum. And Harriet.

Not me!
Gemma

Thanks, Gemma.

If you change your mind, can I have your iTouch?

No, Gemma.

I need some of what he's having ...

RUGBY LESSON NO. 1,000,000,000

Okay, I haven't had a billion rugby
lessons – but it sure feels like it.

I wish Dad would make me play
American football instead.
At least those guys wear some padding.

Marcus, throw the ball!

Not forward!

You can't throw it
forward!

Right. We're supposed to get the ball to the end
to score a try but we're not allowed to pass the
ball forward.

How is that even possible?

Did Coach say 'duck'?

A duck would probably be better at rugby than me.

Coach sent me off for being cheeky.

I sat on the bench trying to think of other cheeky things I could say that would get me sent off more often.

How was I supposed to know that a ruck and a maul are just different ways of fighting for the ball?

69

71

That JT is very scary.

Maybe Spot is right, though. How bad can JT be if he has a pet kitten?

I wonder whether I dare tell the others.

Nope – I'd end up next to the mashed potatoes on his lunch plate.

I guess he might be a bit nicer to me now that I know his secret?

We have a lot in common.
We play rugby.
We have pets.

I guess not! ——

There's another game tomorrow.
We still have sixteen players.

I'm safe.

If you don't play, how will you learn?

Remember Chapter 26...

CHAPTER 26

You learn from LIFE not BOOKS!

Does that mean I don't have to read my History book?

GRRRR!

Maybe the other team will be short of players again!

Didn't Dad see what happened last week?
I'm not worried. I'm sure the other team will bring
enough players. Everyone has heard about Marcus
'Cinderella' Atkinson.

Just for once, I'd like to play a game where everyone speaks English.

Just for once, I'd like to play a computer game.

Just for once, I'd like to play with Harriet and her dolls.

But there I was – going to a rugby game.

The sky was blue.
The sun was shining.
The birds were
singing and the
flowers were
dancing.

So why did I feel like I was going to PUKE???
I hurried around behind the gym. There was no
way I was going be sick in front of all the other
players.

I leaned on the wall and closed my eyes.
Maybe I could just hide?

Maybe I could
pretend my leg
was broken?

Maybe I could send Harriet in to play for me?

Suddenly, I heard voices. Angry voices!

I thought Coach had found me.

I peeked around the corner ...

I told you to get rid of that kitten, JT!

But Fluffy is my pet, Dad!

Fluffy? JT named his kitten Fluffy?

How awful! How can he send Fluffy (Fluffy??) to the RSPCA?

What if someone tried to send Spot away?
How would that make me feel?
Sad, that's how!
And angry ...

CHAPTER
25

Don't get angry, get even.

Poor Fluffy!!
And poor JT.
I could hear him sobbing.
I just hugged Spot and tried not to listen.

80

It's no big deal - who needs a kitten anyway?

He said it – but I didn't believe him. I knew JT was really upset.

It was a good thing that JT and I were on the same team. Otherwise, I'd be in the history books.

HELP!!!

I've just discovered that a really good player can get you mashed even when he's in your team.

Every time JT got the ball, he'd run really close to me ... and then slow down.

Just as the other team got close, he'd pass the ball to me.

You can guess what happened next. YUP. I got mashed.

Spot was so worried he tried to invade the pitch. Dad had to hold on to him.

GRRRRR!

GRRRRR!!

Coach was furious because JT wasn't scoring his usual number of tries.

I guess that's what happens when someone takes your kitten away.

Did I mention that in rugby people injure you on purpose??? I got a cut on my forehead.

The referee wants me in a bin?

I know I'm rubbish at rugby, but there's no reason to be so unpleasant about it.

Apparently you're not allowed on the pitch if you're bleeding. If I'd known that I would have stolen a bottle of tomato sauce from the fridge before the game.

I sat on the bench. Spot licked my hand.

The nurse stuck some
Elastoplast on my head.
I wriggled a lot to make
it difficult. I SO did not
want to get back
on the field.

The whistle blew
for half-time.
Thank goodness.

I saw JT's dad walking to the car. He was holding
Fluffy. JT rugby-tackled him. Well, JT clung to
his ankles.

His dad opened the door and put Fluffy in the car.

He turned around to deal with JT.

And that's when I had my brilliant idea.

BRILLIANT!
JUST BRILLIANT!!
JUST REALLY, REALLY BRILLIANT!!!

JT's dad spotted me!

I ran.
The cat ran.
We didn't stop running till we got back
to the pitch.

I hid Fluffy in my bag. JT came over.

The whistle blew for the start of the second half.

I looked at the score.
Fat chance.

| HOME | 0 |
| AWAY | 26 |

But I'd forgotten how good JT was ...

He caught the ball from a lineout, ran
down the wing and scored a try.

Then he kicked
the conversion.

| HOME | 7 |
| AWAY | 26 |

WOOF!
WOOF!
WOOF!

MeowWWWW!

The ball was coming at me out of the sky.

Catch it, Marcus!

Right.
I'd have better luck catching an eel.

The ball hit me on the head ...

... and bounced to JT.

He caught it!

He avoided all the battering rams!!

He scored!!!

He kicked the conversion!

| HOME | 14 |
| AWAY | 26 |

WOOF! WOOF! WOOF!

MeowWW!

Scrum!

We pushed them over the line!

JT kicked again!!

HOME	21
AWAY	26

One try left to level the match ...
One try left to level the match!!!
ONE TRY!!

JT got the ball. He
ran for the line.

We were going to score.
We were going to SCORE!
WE WERE GOING TO SCORE!!!

Suddenly, he stopped.

The battering rams were
heading for him.

WHAT ARE YOU
DOING???

Coach was red.
Big surprise.

I ran towards JT!

JT! What are you doing? Score! Level the match!

As I got close to him, he threw the ball at me.
I juggled it like a hot potato.

If you drop it, I'll fly you from the school flagpole!

NOW SCORE!!

I gripped the ball as if my life depended on it (it probably did). I flung myself across the line.

Unfortunately,
JT missed the kick.

Level scores.

| HOME | 26 |
| AWAY | 26 |

**Two minutes left.
What now?**

No time for a try. We need a drop goal.

They'll be expecting that.

Not if we give the ball to Marcus...

ARE YOU MAD?

I don't even know what a drop goal is!

**Tank drew a diagram
in the sand.**

Kick it over.

What?

I'll pass you the ball...just kick it over!!

I'm Cinderella!

Remember, she kicked a drop goal with the glass slipper!

Really? I don't remember that.

Maybe rugby kids have different fairytales.

FAIRY TALES for RUGBY KIDS

Contents
· Snow White and the 7 forwards
· Puss in Rugby Boots
· Goldilocks and the 2 flankers
· Jack and the Goal Post.

Okay, I'll do my best.

JT got the ball. He passed it to Tuff. Tuff passed to Tank. All the way down the line.

Then they passed it back the other way ...

My heart was thumping so loud it sounded like a warren of rabbits.

I got the ball.

But I was too close to one of their players.

He charged at me.

I shut my eyes ... put out a hand to hold him off ... dropped the ball.

I swung my foot ...

It went over!
It went over!!
IT WENT OVER!!!

| HOME | 29 |
| AWAY | 26 |

WOOF! WOOF! WOOF! Meooowwww!

The whistle blew!

WE WON!

I SCORED A GOAL!!

THE WINNING GOAL!!!

Were your eyes shut?

I guess it doesn't really matter...

101

The End

103

Have you read my other Diaries?

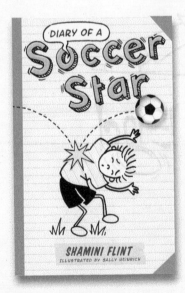